Rocking-Horse Land

For David

K.R.

First Edition   1   2   3   4   5   6   7   8   9   10

Library of Congress Cataloging in Publication Data

Housman, Laurence. 1865-1959. Rocking-horse land / by Laurence Housman; illustrated by Kristina Rodanas.   p.   cm. Summary: Prince Freedling loves the rocking horse he gets for his fifth birthday, but the creature becomes real every night and wants to be set free. ISBN 0-688-09014-1.—ISBN 0-688-09015-X (lib. bdg.) [1. Fairy tales.   2. Rocking horses—Fiction.]   I. Rodanas, Kristina, ill. II. Title. PZ8.H817Ro   1990   [E]—dc20

89-45902 CIP AC

LAURENCE HOUSMAN

Rocking-Horse Land

Illustrated by Kristina Rodanas

Lothrop, Lee & Shepard Books
New York

Little Prince Freedling woke up with a jump and sprang out of bed into the sunshine. He was five years old that morning by all the clocks and calendars in the kingdom; and the day was going to be beautiful. Every golden minute was precious. He was dressed and out of his room before the attendants knew that he was awake.

In the antechamber stood piles on piles of glittering presents; when he walked among them they came up to the measure of his waist. His fairy godmother had sent him a toy with the most humorous effect. It was labeled, "Break me and I shall turn into something else." So every time he broke it, he got a new toy more beautiful than the last. It began by being a hoop, and from that it ran on, while the Prince broke it incessantly for the space of one hour, during which it became by turns—a top, a Noah's ark, a skipping rope, a man-of-war, a box of bricks, a picture puzzle, a pair of stilts, a drum, a trumpet, a kaleidoscope, a steam engine, and nine hundred and fifty other things exactly. Then he began to grow discontented, because it would never turn into the same thing again; and after having broken the man-of-war, he wanted to get it back again. Also he wanted to see if the steam engine would go inside the Noah's ark; but the toy would never be two things at the same time either. This was very unsatisfactory. He thought his fairy godmother ought to have sent him two toys, out of which he could make combinations.

At last he broke it once more, and it turned into a kite; and while he was flying the kite he broke the string, and the kite went sailing away up into nasty blue sky and was never heard of again.

Then Prince Freedling sat down and howled at his fairy godmother; what a dissembling lot fairy godmothers were, to be sure! They were always setting traps to make their godchildren unhappy. Nevertheless, when told to, he took up his pen and wrote her a nice little note, full of bad spelling and tarradiddles, to say what a happy birthday he was spending in breaking up the beautiful toy she had sent him.

Then he went to look at the rest of the presents and found it quite refreshing to break a few that did not send him giddy by turning into anything else.

Suddenly his eyes became fixed with delight; alone, right at the end of the room, stood a great black rocking-horse. The saddle and bridle were hung with tiny gold bells and balls of coral; and the horse's tail and mane flowed till they almost touched the ground.

The Prince scampered across the room and threw his arms around the beautiful creature's neck. All its bells jangled as the head swayed gracefully down; and the prince kissed it between the eyes. Great eyes they were, the color of fire, so wonderfully bright, it seemed they must be really alive, only they did not move, but gazed continually with a set stare at the tapestry-hung wall, on which were figures of armed knights riding to battle.

So Prince Freedling mounted to the back of his rocking-horse; and all day long he rode and shouted to the figures of the armed knights, challenging them to fight, or leading them against the enemy.

At length, when it came to be bedtime, weary of so much glory, he was lifted down from the saddle and carried away to bed.

In his sleep Freedling still felt his black rocking-horse swinging to and fro under him and heard the melodious chime of its bells and, in the land of dreams, saw a great country open before him, full of the sound of the battle cry and the hunting horn calling him to strange perils and triumphs.

In the middle of the night he grew softly awake, and his heart was full of love for his black rocking-horse. He crept gently out of bed: he would go and look at it where it was standing so grand and still in the next room, to make sure that it was all safe and not afraid of being by itself in the dark night. Parting the door hangings he passed through into the wide hollow chamber beyond, all littered about with toys.

The moon was shining through the window, making a square cistern of light upon the floor. And then, all at once, he saw that the rocking-horse had moved from the place where he had left it! It had crossed the room and was standing close to the window with its head toward the night, as though watching the movement of the clouds and the trees swaying in the wind.

The Prince could not understand how it had been moved so; he was a little bit afraid, and stealing timidly across, he took hold of the bridle to comfort himself with the jangle of its bells. As he came close and looked up into the dark solemn face, he saw that the eyes were full of tears and, reaching up, felt one fall warm against his hand.

"Why do you weep, my Beautiful?" said the Prince.

The rocking-horse answered, "I weep because I am a prisoner and not free. Open the window, Master, and let me go!"

"But if I let you go, I shall lose you," said the Prince. "Cannot you be happy here with me!"

"Let me go," said the horse, "for my brothers call me out of Rocking-Horse Land; I hear my mare whinnying to her foals; and they all cry, seeking me through the ups and hollows of my native fastnesses! Sweet Master, let me go this night, and I will return to you when it is day!"

Then Freedling said, "How shall I know that you will return: and what name shall I call you by?"

And the rocking-horse answered, "My name is Rollonde. Search my mane till you find in it a white hair; draw it out and wind it upon one of your fingers; and so long as you have it so wound, you are my master; and wherever I am, I must return at your bidding."

So the Prince drew down the rocking-horse's head, and searching the mane, he found the white hair and wound it upon his finger and tied it. Then he kissed Rollonde between the eyes, saying, "Go, Rollonde, since I love you and wish you to be happy; only return to me when it is day!" And so saying, he threw open the window to the stir of the night.

Then the rocking-horse lifted his dark head and neighed aloud for joy, and swaying forward with a mighty circling motion rose full into the air and sprang out into the free world before him.

Freedling watched how with plunge and curve he went over the bowed trees; and again he neighed into the darkness of the night, then swifter than wind disappeared in the distance. And faintly from far away came a sound of the neighing of many horses answering him.

Then the Prince closed the window and crept back to bed; and all night long he dreamed strange dreams of Rocking-Horse Land. There he saw smooth hills and valleys that rose and sank without a stone or a tree to disturb the steellike polish of their surface, slippery as glass, and driven over by a strong wind; and over them, with a sound like the humming of bees, flew the rocking-horses. Up and down, up and down, with bright manes streaming like colored fires and feet motionless behind and before, went the swift pendulum of their flight. Their long bodies bowed and rose; their heads worked to give impetus to their going; they cried, neighing to each other over hill and valley, "Which of us shall be first? which of us shall be first?" After them the mares with their tall foals came spinning to watch, crying also among themselves, "Ah! which shall be first?"

"Rollonde, Rollonde is first!" shouted the Prince, clapping his hands as they reached the goal; and at that, all at once, he woke and saw it was broad day. Then he ran and threw open the window, and holding out the finger that carried the white hair, cried, "Rollonde, Rollonde, come back, Rollonde!"

Far away he heard an answering sound; and in another moment there came the great rocking-horse himself, dipping and dancing over the hills. He crossed the woods and cleared the palace wall at a bound, and floating in through the window, dropped to rest at Prince Freedling's side, rocking gently to and fro as though panting from the strain of his long flight.

"Now are you happy?" asked the Prince as he caressed him.

"Ah! sweet Prince," said Rollonde, "ah, kind Master!" And then he said no more, but became the stock-still staring rocking-horse of the day before, with fixed eyes and rigid limbs, which could do nothing but rock up and down with a jangling of sweet bells so long as the Prince rode him.

That night Freedling came again when all was still in the palace; and now as before Rollonde had moved from his place and was standing with his head against the window waiting to be let out. "Ah, dear Master," he said, so soon as he saw the Prince coming, "let me go this night also, and surely I will return with day."

So again the Prince opened the window and watched him disappear and heard from far away the neighing of the horses in Rocking-Horse Land calling to him. And in the morning with the white hair round his finger he called, "Rollonde, Rollonde!" and Rollonde neighed and came back to him, dipping and dancing over the hills.

Now this same thing happened every night; and every morning the horse kissed Freedling saying, "Ah! dear Prince and kind Master," and became stock-still once more.

So a year went by, till one morning Freedling woke up to find it was his sixth birthday. And as six is to five, so were the presents he received on his sixth birthday for magnificence and multitude to the presents he had received the year before. His fairy godmother had sent him a bird, a real live bird; but when he pulled its tail it became a lizard, and when he pulled the lizard's tail, it became a mouse, and when he pulled the mouse's tail, it became a cat. Then he did very much want to see if the cat would eat the mouse, and not being able to have them both he got rather vexed with his fairy godmother. However, he pulled the cat's tail, and the cat became a dog, and when he pulled the dog's, the dog became a goat; and so it went on till he got to a cow. And he pulled the cow's tail and it became a camel, and he pulled the camel's tail and it became an elephant, and still not being contented, he pulled the elephant's tail and it became a guinea pig. Now a guinea pig has no tail to pull, so it remained a guinea pig, while Prince Freedling sat down and howled at his fairy godmother.

But the best of all his presents was the one given to him by the King his father. It was a most beautiful horse, for, said the King, "You are now old enough to learn to ride."

So Freedling was put upon the horse's back, and from having ridden so long upon his rocking-horse he learned to ride perfectly in a single day and was declared by all the courtiers to be the most perfect equestrian that was ever seen.

Now these praises and the pleasure of riding a real horse so occupied his thoughts that that night he forgot all about Rollonde, and falling fast asleep, dreamed of nothing but real horses and horsemen going to battle. And so it was the next night too.

But the night after that, just as he was falling asleep, he heard someone sobbing by his bed, and a voice saying, "Ah! dear Prince and kind Master, let me go, for my heart breaks for a sight of my native land." And there stood his poor rocking-horse Rollonde, with tears falling out of his beautiful eyes onto the white coverlet.

Then the Prince, full of shame at having forgotten his friend, sprang up and threw his arms round his neck saying, "Be of good cheer, Rollonde, for now surely I will let thee go!" and he ran to the window and opened it for the horse to go through. "Ah, dear Prince and kind Master!" said Rollonde. Then he lifted his head and neighed so that the whole palace shook, and swaying forward till his head almost touched the ground, he sprang out into the night and away toward Rocking-Horse Land.

Then Prince Freedling, standing by the window, thoughtfully unloosed the white hair from his finger and let it float into the darkness, out of sight of his eye or reach of his hand.

"Good-bye, Rollonde," he murmured softly, "brave Rollonde, my own good Rollonde! Go and be happy in your own land, since I, your Master, was forgetting to be kind to you." And far away he heard the neighing of horses in Rocking-Horse Land.

Many years after, when Freedling had become King in his father's stead, the fifth birthday of the Prince his son came to be celebrated; and there on the morning of the day, among all the presents that covered the floor of the chamber, stood a beautiful foal rocking-horse, black, with deep-burning eyes.

No one knew how it had come there or whose present it was, till the King himself came to look at it. And when he saw it so like the old Rollonde he had loved as a boy, he smiled and, stroking its dark mane, said softly in its ear, "Art thou, then, the son of Rollonde?" And the foal answered him, "Ah, dear Prince and kind Master!" but never a word more.

Then the King took the little Prince his son and told him the story of Rollonde as I have told it here; and at the end he went and searched in the foal's mane till he found one white hair, and drawing it out, he wound it about the little Prince's finger, bidding him guard it well and be ever a kind master to Rollonde's son.

So here is my story of Rollonde come to a good ending.